MYSTERIOUS MONSTERS

BOOK 1:

BIGFOOT

COMING TO A BASEMENT NEAR YOU

Mysterious Monsters: Bigfoot

For more information, to inquire about rights to this or other works, or to purchase copies for special educational, business, or sales promotional uses please write to:

Corgi Bits is an imprint of Incorgnito Publishing Press
A division of Market Management Group, LLC
300 E. Bellevue Drive, Suite 208
Pasadena, California 91101

FIRST EDITION

Printed in the United States of America

ISBN: 978-1-944589-23-3

10 9 8 7 6 5 4 3 2 1

For my students

Contents

INTRODUCTION

BIGFOOT

Dear Readers,

At night, when you call your mom and dad into the spooky darkness of your room, is it to have them *open* your closet? Are you the type to leave a dish of chocolate chip cookies under your bed, with a sign reading, "There's more where these came from"? Do you cry your eyes out at the end of monster movies, when the poor, innocent, man-munching creature dies?

If the answer to these questions is yes, then read on, because the story of the mysterious Mattigan monsters is most definitely for you. If not, then perhaps it might be best to tuck this book away. Maybe put it on your baby sister's bookshelf. Go ahead and pick up her glow-in-the-dark, scratch-and-snort edition of "The Fuzzy Little Unicorn Who Pooped Rainbows," instead.

Because this book, and those that follow, are about things that could eat and poop *you*. They're about three kids, the Mattigans, who do some awfully strange things. For example, when they learn that mysterious monsters might really exist, they don't hide under their covers with their fingers in their ears, humming the "Rainbow Poop" song.

Instead, *they go looking for them.*

Which is especially tricky, since it's their father's job to prove that people who say things like "mysterious monsters exist," are liars.

Still here?

Excellent, you don't scare easy.

Let's begin, then, with how it all began, in a big house at the edge of a forest — in Oregon.

CHAPTER ONE

AN INTERESTING FAMILY

"Theo!" Maddie called. "Where are you? The sitter's here, and Dad has to go! Come say goodbye!" She was using her twelve-year-old-big-sister-boss voice. Maddie not-so-secretly liked being in charge. But with no mom and two rascals for little brothers, she often had no choice, anyway.

"On it!" said Max, the shaggy-haired, ten-year-old, middle Mattigan brother. He grabbed his extendable "spy-nocular" from his spy kit and got into "the crouch," which he thought made him look dramatic when he was in search mode. Even though it was hard to get around that way, he began crouching in and out of the many rooms on the bottom floor of the Mattigan Mansion.

Technically, it was a mansion because it was huge. It

had dozens of rooms sprawling across three floors and a massive, maze-like basement. But it wasn't the least bit fancy. In fact, it was old and sort of falling apart. The kids didn't mind, though, because they weren't fancy types.

Marcus Mattigan, the kids' dad, stood at the open front door with his travel bag at his feet. The tall, green trees of Portland's Forest Park stood shoulder to shoulder behind him. Their tops looked a lot like his: capped with wild tufts of upswept hair. "Theo!" he called, "I'm in a hurry!"

The kids' sitter stood next to him, holding her bag. She was a small lady with wrinkled, but rosy cheeks, and kind eyes. Maddie was sure the poor woman was in for a hard time. "He's probably hiding somewhere watching "Hansel and Gretel" again," she explained. "Even though he knows perfectly well our dad doesn't approve of fairy tales about made-up — "

"Ah-*ha!*" Max had crouched into the living room and sniffed his way over to the two giant built-in benches that ran under the giant windows, which made up almost the whole side of the house. The side-by-side

benches were both big enough to hide two Theos, so
Max tapped along them with his spy-nocular, hoping
to make his prey give itself away. When he thought he
heard chewing, he pointed triumphantly to the bench
on the right.

Everyone went over. Marcus lifted the seat.

Eight-year-old, mop-topped Theo Mattigan was
curled up on pillows deep inside the tunnel-like bench,
munching a peanut-butter-and-banana sandwich. He
had a sack full of peanut-butter-and-banana sandwiches in there with him, because he never went anywhere
without a sack full of peanut-butter-and-banana sandwiches. He was watching something on his phone.

When Theo finally looked up, his eyes bugged out.
He shoved the phone into the pillows, but it was too late.

"Theo," Maddie sighed, pulling the ear buds out
from under her brother's heap of hair. "The Madam
Blavatsky Hour? That phony psychic's show was *cancelled* because of Dad! *Teachable Moment!"* she declared.
Their father was big on delivering on-the-spot life les-
sons. "Her husband, Ivan, cyber-stalked her clients so

they'd believe in the strange voices he made from under her crystal-ball table!"

Marcus took a deep breath.

"I know Dad proved she was a faker!" Theo promised. "I know people can't really talk to you from the future! And I know ghosts and vampires and haunted houses aren't real! I'm just — wouldn't it be neat if they *were?*" Then he gulped, and blurted, "I think *this* house is haunted!"

"Really, Theo?" Max said, rolling his eyes.

Marcus took another deep breath. "Theo," he said calmly, "the *real* world is amazing enough without making up fantastic — "

"Humph!" Theo protested. "I'm gonna lock the sitter in a haunted basement room, anyway."

"Theo!" everyone yelped, completely embarrassed. "The sitter is right here!"

"Oops," Theo said. "Here." He held out a bitten sandwich wedge to her as a peace offering.

"It's okay, really," the sitter said, chuckling. "You

13

can call me Betsy."

"*If* that's your real name," Max said, looking at her face through the spy-nocular.

"Actually, my real name is Elizabeth."

"Ah-*ha!*"

"And you were using Dad's account!" Maddie realized, ignoring Max's usual nonsense. She'd fished Theo's phone out of the bench. "His records show what he orders," she explained to Betsy, and then went back to scolding Theo: "Dad's a famous *skeptic!* Can you imagine how damaging it would be for him if the world thought he was watching The Madam — "

"It's fine, Maddie," Marcus interrupted. "I often watch those kind of shows to see what the latest hoaxes are. In fact, just this morning I saw one about Area 51 in Nevada. Someone is claiming that the alien the government has supposedly been hiding there for over fifty years has escaped and is running around the desert. So now, of course, people are rushing there from all over the country to catch it."

"People," Maddie, Max, Theo and Marcus all sighed.

"Is that where you're going, Dad?" Max asked. "To prove it's all a fake?"

"No," Marcus said. "I'm going to West Virginia, to do a show about a silly legend they call the Mothman. It's a seven-foot-tall flying creature with red eyes that glow in the dark. Locals are claiming to have seen it lately."

"People," the Mattigans all sighed again.

"'Course, all I need to catch it is a really big flashlight," Marcus added. He waited a second, then said, "See what I did there? *Moth*man? Really big *flashlight?"*

His kids just stared at him.

Maddie turned to Betsy and said, "We apologize in advance for our father's sense of humor."

"Sigh," Marcus said. "And I apologize in advance for my children's lack of funny bones. They were removed after a tragic accident with a car full of clowns. Very sad. Hilarious, though."

"You guys are an interesting family," Betsy said.

"True story!" the Mattigan kids enthusiastically agreed.

CHAPTER TWO

AN UNEXPECTED GUEST

Marcus gave the kids each a hug, then said, "You guys know the getting-along rules — "

The Mattigan kids all sang out:

"Notta fist!"

"Notta foot!"

"Notta finger!"

"In which case — " Marcus replied.

"Notta problem!"

"Oklahoma, then."

"Do they often speak at the same time?" Betsy asked.

"No," the kids all replied.

"I wouldn't take their word for it," Marcus said, shouldering his bag. And then, finally, he turned and left.

"Here," Theo said, offering Betsy the sandwich wedge again.

"Thank you, dear. But, no, thank you."

"Not everyone likes peanut butter and banana, Theo," Maddie pointed out.

"Humph!"

"I'll just head upstairs and unpack," Betsy told the kids. "Then I'll come back down, and maybe we can have some fun! To me, this house looks perfect for Hide-and-Go-Seek. But then again, I'd be afraid no one would ever find me!"

"We love that game," Maddie said, trying to be accommodating. When her brothers didn't say anything, she Eyeballed them.

"True story!" they finally agreed. They hated getting Eyeballed, especially about manners, but Hide-and-Go-Seek actually was one of their favorite games. And the Mattigan Mansion *was* the best Hide-and-Go-Seek house in the world.

"Alrighty then," Betsy said, heading upstairs. "You're on."

When she was out of sight, the kids looked at each other.

"This might actually be fun," Maddie said, then immediately began the process of wrangling her untamable tangle of frizzy black hair. It often gave her away in games of Hide-and-Go-Seek.

But then the doorbell rang.

"*On it!*" Max announced, already crouching toward the door in full-on spy mode. Theo hurried after him, excited for the show.

"*Max,*" Maddie warned, following him for the opposite reason. "People don't like it when you — "

"Ah-*ha!*" Max cried, whipping the door open.

Standing on the welcome mat was a startled old man in a fancy, but rumpled coat and tie. He looked ill, leaning on a cane while trying to hold onto both a video camera and a thick, disorderly book of some kind. Its pages were held together with fraying twine and scruffy rubber bands.

"Oh, my goodness!" the old man exclaimed, when he'd recovered from the shock of Max's greeting. "Look at that hair! It's just like your father's!"

All three Mattigan kids narrowed their eyes. They loved their Mattigan mops and didn't tolerate anyone making fun of them. But before they got the chance to say so, the old man added, "It's just like your mother's, too!"

"But — " Maddie sputtered, taken completely off guard. "Our — our mom vanished. Two years ago!"

"I know, poor children," the old man said. "I know! But not *all* missing family members need to be missing forever, and I am living proof! I'm your long-lost Grandpa Joe!"

CHAPTER THREE

THE MONSTER JOURNAL

Grandpa Joe hobbled into the house while the Mattigan kids stood staring at each other with their mouths hanging open. They'd never laid eyes on Grandpa Joe in their lives. They'd never even seen pictures. He made his shuffling way to the puffy couch in the living room and collapsed onto it. With a bit of a groan, he set his book and video camera on the coffee table.

The kids remained standing at the door until, finally, Theo said, "But you weren't long lost. Dad hates you."

"Theo Mattigan!" Maddie snapped, jolted out of her daze. "That's just plain rude!"

"*Humph!*"

Maddie cautiously approached Grandpa Joe, so her brothers followed. He looked terribly weak and weary. No one knew what to say.

"I earned your father's hatred," Grandpa Joe admitted. "I was hoping to speak with him about that very thing. It's been too long — far, far too long. Is he here?"

"He just went out of town," Maddie said. "He won't be back until later in the week."

"I'm so sorry to hear that." Grandpa Joe let out a long, disappointed sigh.

"Why did you leave him?" Max demanded, anyway. "He was only a kid — like us! It's no fun having a missing parent!" He glared at Maddie, daring her to call him rude.

She didn't though, because she wanted to hear the answer.

All three Mattigan kids stood there waiting to hear it.

"I have no excuse," Grandpa Joe told the kids. "But I do have a reason." He gestured weakly to the book on the coffee table. "It's my journal," he added. "Have a look."

Max couldn't help but approach the battered bundle of pages. He loved books, especially *old* books, the more beat-up the better. His favorite thing in the world, besides spying, of course, was searching for cool used books at garage sales with his dad — which felt a bit like spying, actually. His room was positively bursting with their finds.

As Max carefully removed the twine and rubber bands from the journal, Maddie and Theo moved behind him to look over his shoulder. There was nothing on the dirty cover, so he gently turned it over. Sloppy writing on the first page said, "Mysterious Monsters." He turned a few more pages and found an entry on werewolves. There was a drawing of a vicious, human-like wolf with dripping fangs. Page two had maps and all kinds of notes scribbled by hand. Max loved maps, too.

"Gross," Maddie said. Theo's eyes were as big as saucers.

Max turned the page to reveal a ghost, but this was not the cute and friendly cartoon type. It was a frightening black shadow with a devilish grin. There was a creature on every pair of pages: Sasquatches and vampires and aliens. It seemed there was a page for just about every creature from every nightmare the kids had ever had. When Max got to the end of the book, all three Mattigans looked up, having completely forgotten where they were.

"What do you make of it?" Grandpa Joe asked.

"Awesome," said Theo.

Max said only, *"Well — "*

"Very imaginative," Maddie admitted. "But we'd rather read a book about real animals, so that we can learn something useful."

"I swear to you," said Grandpa Joe, "that every monster in that journal is one-hundred-percent real. I have spent a lifetime gathering the evidence on those pages. Unfortunately, I have never been able to prove the existence of monsters by actually *finding* one." He looked even more tired now.

"Is this why you left Dad?" Maddie asked. "To search for these monsters?"

"Indeed," Grandpa Joe confirmed. "I became obsessed with crypto-zoology, the study of mysterious creatures, and it cost me my family. Over the years, I considered giving up the search many times, but then I decided that if I searched just one more year, I would find *one* monster, and then your father would understand. And he would forgive me."

None of the kids knew what to say to this. Now they all felt sad for Grandpa Joe, but they were still mad at him. They were also beginning to understand why their father was so serious about not wasting time on imaginary things.

"May I tell you the *real* reason I came here today?" asked Grandpa Joe. He was leaning back on the couch now, looking weaker by the moment.

The kids nodded.

"I've been waiting for your father to leave. It's *you* I wanted to see. I was hoping you kids might help me."

"Find these made-up monsters?" Maddie asked. "But you know very well that Dad is a famous — "

"Just one," Grandpa Joe said, softly. It came out

almost in a whisper. "Just one would show him that I wasn't crazy and didn't waste my life."

Maddie's outrage fizzled. Seeing this, her brothers' did, too.

The three Mattigan kids looked at each other, unsure of what to do now.

"What's going on, kids?" Betsy suddenly called down from the staircase's second-floor landing. She'd been coming back down, but stopped when she saw Joe. "Do you have a visitor?"

"It's our Grandpa Joe!" Theo announced.

"*If* that's his real name!"

"Max!" Maddie Eyeballed her brother, but she knew it was a waste of time. "I'm really sorry," she said, turning to Grandpa Joe.

"Actually," Grandpa Joe said, "my real name is Joseph."

"Ah-*ha!*"

"Well, this is wonderful!" Betsy said, hurrying down the rest of the stairs. When she came into the

26

living room, she looked at Joe with concern. "Will you be staying over?" she asked him. "You look positively exhausted."

Grandpa Joe turned to Maddie with hopeful eyes. She turned to her brothers to find them looking at her in exactly the same way.

It took a few moments, but Maddie made a decision that changed the fate of the Mattigan family forever. "Yes," she said to Betsy. "Grandpa Joe will be staying with us for a few days. We're helping him prepare a surprise for our dad."

CHAPTER FOUR

THE BICKERING

"Then I'll just go right back upstairs and prepare a room for him," Betsy said. And with that, she was gone again.

"Bless you!" Grandpa Joe said to the kids. "If there was a page in my journal for angels, the three of you would be on it!"

"It doesn't mean we're going to help you look for those silly monsters," Maddie warned.

"You wouldn't deny an old man's dying wish, would you?"

"Dying!" the kids all gasped.

"Soon," Grandpa Joe said. "I don't know how much time I have left, but I fear it's not much. But never mind all that: It's the Sasquatch we must find. The Bigfoot! It has been seen in the Northwest many, many times. I have tracked it here! To Forest Park! That is why I have come!"

"We'll help you get upstairs for some rest," Maddie said, Eyeballing her brothers into action. "That's all we can promise right now."

Grandpa Joe nodded. Max and Theo helped him up, and then they got him to the second floor bedroom that Betsy was making up for him. Then they rushed back down to Maddie.

That's when the bickering began.

"He's awesome!" Theo proclaimed, already turning pages in the monster journal, looking for the Bigfoot entry.

"He's crazy," was Maddie's opinion.

"He's *dying*," Max pointed out.

"Wow!" Theo cried when he found the right page. "'A giant, ape-like creature covered in thick hair!' Kinda like us! Except for the giant part. And it's here, in our forest!"

"It's our duty to carry out his last wish, even *if* he's crazy," Max argued. He didn't believe for a second that any of the monsters in that journal were real, but since their dad wasn't around, he couldn't think of a better way to spend a Saturday afternoon than trying to find one. He felt the crouch coming on.

"Teachable Moment," Maddie declared. "It's our *duty* to take care of him."

Theo kept staring at the Sasquatch entry. "It can weigh up to 500 pounds!" he read. "I want one!"

"Teachable Moment yourself!" Max shot back. "Searching for Sasquatch *would* be taking care of him. It's his final wish!"

Maddie was exasperated. "We're not running around the woods looking for Bigfoot!"

"Why not?" Max demanded. "Just for fun! Just to make him feel better!"

"Because — it's — absurd! Besides, what would we tell Betsy? And Dad would — !"

"He'll *leave* if we don't help!"

"So?"

"We need him to stay until Dad gets home! So they can make up!"

This stumped Maddie. She wasn't convinced, but that was the most genuinely thoughtful thing her brother had ever said. In fact, now that she thought about it, that might have been the *first* genuinely thoughtful thing he had ever —

"Where's Theo?" Max wondered, interrupting Maddie's thoughts.

"What do you mean?" Maddie asked. "Oh, no — "

The littlest Mattigan was no longer there, and the front door was wide open.

CHAPTER FIVE

THE WRONG HUNT

Maddie sprinted to the door and desperately scanned the edge of the woods. "Theo!" she shouted. "Theo!" She looked around, unsure of what to do. "He took Grandpa Joe's video camera," she said, seeing it was gone. "And the monster journal! And I still have his phone!"

Max opened the bench his brother had been hiding in. "The little bugger took his sandwich sack, too," he said. "Spilled a bunch, though."

"Come on," Maddie sighed. "We need to track him down before he gets lost."

"On it." Max scooped up his spy kit and rushed straight outside.

"Betsy!" Maddie shouted up to the second floor. "We're — we're going out for a walk in the woods! But not very far! Don't worry! We do it all the time! We'll be back soon!" Before Betsy could say anything — like no or that she wanted to go with them — Maddie hurried outside. Max was already crouching for the tree line. She sighed, then set off after him.

The Mattigan kids knew the woods around their house very well, since they played there almost every day in the summertime. Maddie and Max sprinted up and down their familiar trails, calling their brother's name. Max scanned for Theo with his spy-nocular, but soon enough, it became clear that Theo had gone farther into the woods than he was allowed.

Tears filled Maddie's eyes as she and Max left the trails and wove through the trees, jumping over fallen branches and shoving aside bushes. It had been *her* decision to let Grandpa Joe stay. She shouldn't have let her brothers even consider going on such a ridiculous wild goose chase. And now, her baby brother was gone. She would never, ever be able to face their father if anything happened to Theo.

Up ahead, Max suddenly stopped running. "Keep going!" Maddie yelled. "We have to — !"

But now Max was kneeling down with his magnifying glass, looking at something on the ground. Maddie stopped when she reached him, panting. "What is it?" she asked, trying to catch her breath. "Did you find some kind of clue?"

Max picked something up and showed it to her. "A bite-sized bit of peanut-butter-and-banana sandwich," he said.

"He's eating even while wandering the woods in search of Sasquatch?"

"Look!" Max hurried a few paces ahead and knelt down again. He'd spotted another sandwich bit. He stood up with it. "What's that kooky kid doing?" he asked, turning back to Maddie. "Maybe there's a hole in his bag."

For a moment, he and his sister just stared at each other, wondering. Then they got it.

"A trail of breadcrumbs!" they cried.

"It's from Hansel and Gretel!" Max realized. "Theo's leaving a trail so he can find his way back!" Max was incredibly relieved, because even though he loved a good spy search, he didn't love a good spy search for a lost little brother.

"But this is the *woods!*" Maddie complained. *"Real* woods, not fairy tale woods!" The excitement of solving the mini-mystery had worn off almost immediately. "There are *animals* out here! Doesn't he realize his trail is going to be *eaten?"*

Max and Maddie knew they had to hurry, so they searched wildly for more sandwich bits. Fortunately, they weren't hard to find. The little chunks created a long, zigzagging path through the trees. Max led the way in his crouch, following the trail.

At the top of a steep hill, they finally spotted their brother. He was at the bottom on the other side, standing still as a statue in a small clearing.

"Theo!" Maddie called, but his back was turned, and he didn't react. *"Theo!"*

"If that's your real name!"

"I'm sure he can hear us," Maddie said. "He's just being stubborn. Stay right there!" she hollered to Theo, wishing she could Eyeball the little chump. "We're coming to get you!"

Theo *still* didn't react. He was just standing there like he'd been turned to stone, looking at his feet. Actually, they realized as they picked their way down the hill, he was pointing Grandpa Joe's video camera at his feet.

"He probably found some disgusting bug or something," Maddie guessed. When they reached the little troublemaker, she grabbed the camera out of his hand and put its strap over her head. Then she launched right into Lecture Mode. "Teachable Moment, Theo Mattigan!" she ranted. "You had us scared to death! Do you know how worried we were? Who do you think you are, going off all by yourself like that? Do you realize what could have happened to — ?"

"Uh, Maddie?" Max interrupted.

"What!"

"Look."

Max was pointing to the ground around Theo's feet, at the same thing Theo hadn't stopped staring at even after his camera was snatched away.

"Crikey," Maddie said.

Theo was standing in a gigantic footprint.

CHAPTER SIX

EVIDENCE

"Is that what it looks like?" Maddie whispered. *"It can't be."*

"Are there any more?" Max asked, whispering, too.

Theo pointed. There were lots of gigantic footprints — lots and lots of them. They were all over the little clearing.

"It just can't be," Maddie whispered again. But there they were, in plain sight: footprints several times too large to be human. Maddie wasn't ready to believe her own eyes, so she turned back to Theo. "Don't you realize that animals will eat your sandwich bits?" she asked, already forgetting the urge to keep her voice down. "If they're gone, who knows how long it'll take us to find our way back!"

Theo interrupted — by handing Maddie the monster journal, which was folded over at the Sasquatch page. "Teachable Moment," he said, pointing to something on one of the pages without looking away from the footprint.

"The best evidence of Sasquatch activity is large footprints," Maddie read. "But there are other signs. The most important is that normal wildlife activity in the area will cease. Animals will have been scared away."

Max and Maddie looked around, listening hard. The woods were silent.

"I don't think we've seen any animals," Max said. "Have we?"

"I'm not sure," Maddie admitted. "I don't think I have. But that doesn't actually mean — "

"Shhh," Theo said.

All three kids went quiet again, listening even harder. Max scanned the area with his spy-nocular.

They heard something. A rustling.

"Video camera," Theo whispered.

Maddie, her heart suddenly pounding, lifted the camera, which was still on, and pointed it briefly at the footprint he was standing in. Then she swept it over the ground around them to get the others. *"I really can't believe I'm saying this,"* she whispered into the microphone, *"but we seem to have discovered a whole bunch of Sasquatch footprints. They're enormous! But I'm positive there's a logical explanation for —"*

"Shhh!"

"Theo," Maddie said, filming the tree line now, "we need to think this through. Like Dad always says, things aren't always what they appear —"

"Shhh!"

All three kids went silent one more time. Max scanned. Maddie filmed, looking for the logical explanation she was sure they'd find, if they would just calm down.

Suddenly, they heard loud crunching in the underbrush.

And then they saw it.

CHAPTER SEVEN

THE CHASE

"SASQUAAAAATCH!" Max screamed. He didn't mean to — it just slipped out. Everyone saw it: a furry head in the distance, just visible through the screen of branches and leaves.

But now it was moving away from them — fast.

All at once, the three Mattigan kids lost their minds. Or showed their true colors. Or both.

Whatever the case, they chased after it.

Maddie took the lead. She was the fastest and had the camera, which she aimed at the bobbing head that sporadically appeared and disappeared from her line of sight.

Max was in hot pursuit behind Maddie, and Theo did his best to keep up with him.

At one point, Maddie lost sight of the furry figure altogether.

The kids stopped to catch their breath.

"Dad is going to be so happy!" Max panted, his hands on his knees. "We're gonna catch a Sasquatch for him, and that's gonna disprove the biggest lie in his life — that his father doesn't love him!"

"That way!" Theo screamed when a rustle sounded from their left.

And they were off again.

All three Mattigans got scraped and bruised barging through the brush. Maddie dropped the camera once, but luckily it only fell against her chest. Max dropped his spy kit and had to stop to pick it back up. Theo tripped and fell several times — though he never came close to losing hold of his sandwich sack.

The three of them ran in frantic pursuit of that bobbing head of hair. But they just couldn't catch up to it, and eventually they grew too tired to continue. Finally, they gave up, collapsing onto a pile of soft green leaves. The trio lay there until they recovered enough to sit up and look at each other.

They grinned.

"Did you get it?" Max asked Maddie. "Tell me you got it."

The boys gathered round as Maddie played the footage back. It was hard to see anything clearly with the camera shaking like crazy, but the hairy head was, at times, visible — sort of.

"Not very convincing," Maddie concluded.

"I'm convinced!"

"You can't be convinced without *convincing* proof, Theo. Dad has told you that a million times. *Major* Teachable — "

"Humph! On *yumpf!"*

"Kids," Maddie sighed.

"It doesn't matter," Max said. "Bigfoot is here — in Forest Park. And we're going to find him."

"Tomorrow," Maddie told him. "It's going to get dark soon, and Betsy is probably freaking out right now. And I'm not even sure where we are. If we *really* think we saw — "

"We saw!" the Mattigan boys insisted.

"Okay," Maddie allowed. "Okay. But we need to go home and come up with a plan, a real, thoughtful, organized *plan*. We need to sleep on it." She always thought more clearly after a good night's rest.

"How will we find our way back here?" Max asked. Then he and Maddie turned to their little brother. "Theo?" they prompted.

"If that's my real name!" Theo said, beating Max to the punch. He took a sandwich out of his sack and started tearing off bits of it.

The kids immediately began picking their way back through the woods, leaving a long trail of peanut-butter-and-banana bits behind them. It took almost an hour, but just as it was starting to get dark, they stumbled on Theo's first trail and followed it back to the mansion.

Despite how tired they were, the kids ran up onto the porch and then into the house. They sprinted straight up to Grandpa Joe's room, where they found him awake, but looking drained. He was sweating as profusely as they were, if not worse.

"We saw it!" Theo blurted. "We chased it! We saw it, and we chased it all over the place!"

Grandpa Joe's grin was so big that it made all three Mattigans smile right along with him. *"Did you — did you — the camera?"* he croaked.

"We got some shots of his head," Maddie said. "No *real* proof — but we're going to make a new plan in the morning. Are — are you okay?"

"Yes, dear. Just running a slight fever — nothing to worry about. Please, tell me more."

"We'll find him," Max promised. "And we'll show Dad when he gets home. And you'll be friends again."

"Bless you children," Grandpa Joe said. "Do you think you could leave the camera with me? I would so dearly love to see what you saw."

"Of course," Maddie said, handing it over. "It's your camera, after all. I just wish the footage was better."

"No matter," Grandpa Joe said. "It sounds wonderfully promising."

"We'd better go make sure Betsy knows we're okay," Maddie said, certain their sitter must be furious with them by now. "We'll see you in the morning, okay?"

"Actually, kids," Grandpa Joe said. "Betsy left."

"She *left?*" all three kids asked, unsure they'd heard correctly.

"She got an emergency call from another family she sits for," Grandpa Joe explained. "Of course she said she was booked, but I told her that I was perfectly capable of watching you. I promised her I'd be feeling much better by morning, so she took the other job. They were really quite desperate."

The kids looked at each other, each thinking the exact same thing: their search for the Sasquatch would be much easier now.

"Our search for the Sasquatch will be much easier now," Grandpa Joe said.

"True story!" the kids all agreed.

"Good night, then, my angels," said Grandpa Joe. "We'll get on it first thing in the morning."

"Good night, Grandpa Joe."

The kids slipped out of the room. In the hall, they looked at one another in a way they never had before. Then they all hugged. It was a first. Then they headed off to bed.

Even though it was barely eight o'clock, the Mattigan kids were asleep almost before their heads hit their pillows.

CHAPTER EIGHT

BIG-TIME TROUBLE

Maddie woke up the next morning and looked at her clock, amazed to see how long she'd slept in. It was almost eleven o'clock. She found her brothers in Max's room, hunkered down on the floor in the midst of his piles of books. Max's prized possessions were always spilling off his bookshelves and lying all over — everything. He and Theo had made some space for themselves to pore over a map of the woods that they'd drawn. They were making plans for a hunt.

"I'll go check on Grandpa Joe," Maddie told them, then headed to his room.

Max and Theo continued swapping theories about where Bigfoot's nest would be. They found some helpful information in the journal. It said Sasquatches would look to bed down in hidden gaps in an area's densest growth.

"Max! Theo!" Maddie called. "Come quick!"

The boys jumped up and ran.

"Is he okay?" Max cried when they burst into Grandpa Joe's room.

Maddie was just standing there, looking worried. "He's gone!" she cried.

"What do you mean he's gone?" Max asked. The bed was empty and unmade, but that didn't seem like a big deal. The bathroom door was open, though, and he could see that was empty, too.

"I don't understand," Maddie said, mostly to herself. "I checked around the whole floor — downstairs, too. Why would he leave without telling us?"

"He's playing Hide-and-Go-Seek!" Theo decided. "I bet he went down to the basement!"

"Without his cane?"

It was on the bed. Max went over to have a look, but nothing about it seemed to provide any clues. Underneath it was a stack of tabloid newspapers, the kind announcing in gigantic letters that aliens walked among us. In fact, the headline on the top newspaper said exactly that. It was about the supposed escape outside of Las Vegas. The one under that said Sasquatch walked among us.

"His research?" Max guessed.

"Maybe," Maddie said. "Where's his camera?"

The kids looked around the room. There was no sign of it.

No one knew what to think.

They searched all the places where Grandpa Joe might have left them a note: on their bedroom doors, on the puffy couch by the coffee table in the living room, on the front door — but there was nothing.

"Olly, olly, oxen free!" Theo called down the basement steps.

But no one came out of hiding.

"Let's eat breakfast and talk about this," Maddie suggested. She always thought best on a full stomach.

In the kitchen, Max and Maddie poured themselves cereal, while Theo made a peanut-butter-and-banana sandwich.

The three kids ate while staring at one another, confused and concerned.

"Maybe he went out to get some more footage," Max finally suggested. "Sasquatches get up early."

"That would explain not leaving a note," said Maddie.

"But not the cane."

"Right," Maddie agreed. "Good point, Theo."

"Maybe he took the video to be authenticated," Max tried.

"But it was our footage," said Maddie.

"But it was his camera," said Max.

"Still."

"The cane?"

"Theo's right," Maddie admitted. "Maybe we should call Dad and tell him what's going on. I mean, what if something's happened to him? It's Dad's *father* we're talking about here. And now we have no babysitter! Shall we vote?"

Max put up his foot.

Maddie put up her fist.

Theo put up his finger.

"It's decided, then," Maddie said. She'd left her cell phone in her room, so she went and got the landline phone on the counter. It's voicemail light was blinking, which surprised her. "There's a message from Dad," she said, alarmed at the numbers blinking on the readout. "From yesterday, at two in the morning!" She clicked "play," and put the phone to her ear.

Both Max and Theo, who'd gone back to eating, stopped mid-chew when they saw her face turn white.

Maddie put the phone down and said, "Get the laptop. We're in big-time trouble."

Max got the laptop.

"Search 'Mattigan Sasquatch,'" Maddie said. Her voice was shaking.

"What's going on?" Max asked.

"I sense a Teachable Moment coming on," Theo moaned.

"A bad one."

"No, really," Max pressed. "What's going on?"

"We are idiots," Maddie groaned. *"That's* what's going on.' Dad's on his way home."

Links popped up to videos. Max clicked the first one.

A window opened and a video started playing. Grandpa Joe was on it, smiling in a shockingly evil way. He didn't look the least bit sick, either. In fact, he looked much younger and full of energy. Next to him was a woman they all recognized at once.

All three Mattigans felt like throwing up.

"My name is Madam Blavatsky," said the disgraced psychic. "I once had big career helping many thousands of people to feel better about their miserable lives by predicting better futures for them. Only until Marcus Mattigan ruined my life by telling whole world I am fraud! Well, my husband Ivan and I are here to tell you: Marcus Mattigan is fraud! While he goes on the TV claiming monsters are fake, he has his own children searching for Sasquatch! Look at this!"

On came the kids' footage. First were shots of the giant footprints, then Maddie's voice was heard, saying, "We seem to have discovered a whole bunch of Sasquatch footprints. They're enormous!"

"That's not all I said!" Maddie protested. "I said I couldn't believe — !"

The Blavastkys came back on. *"I made enormous footprints!"* Ivan cackled, showing off a pole with a giant fake foot attached to it. He laughed like a madman.

"Humph on yumpf!" Theo shouted.

Then there was the shaky footage Maddie shot running through the woods. The screen froze on a good look at the back of the furry head.

"Fake Bigfoot head on stick!" Madam Blavatsky roared, coming back on and showing the other end of her husband's pole, which had the head on it. "Revenge is tasting sweet!"

Max and Maddie groaned. The head didn't look real at all.

The kids' footage played again, and then Max was

saying, "Dad is going to be so happy! We're gonna catch a Sasquatch for him, and that's gonna disprove the biggest lie in his life — !"

"They took a part out!" Max raged. "THAT'S NOT FAIR!"

The video ended with both of the Blavatskys laughing like lunatics.

The kids saw that it had over one hundred thousand hits already.

Max closed the laptop.

The Mattigan children went silent, painfully, sickly silent — until Maddie finally said, "Dad's producer cancelled the investigation he was doing in West Virginia."

She was on the verge of tears.

"They're temporarily suspending his show," she continued, barely holding it together. "Dad's entire career is based on people trusting him — and now there are thousands of angry comments on that video, calling him a phony! Because of us! He said he was taking the first flight home. He could be here any time now. He's very upset."

Then she lost it.

When Max and Theo saw their sister crying, they lost it, too. Maddie Mattigan never cried.

And then the front door slammed open.

CHAPTER NINE

ANOTHER UNEXPECTED GUEST

The kids rushed out of the kitchen — afraid, but anxious to explain everything to their father. But they stopped dead the moment they reached the front door. Once again, it wasn't their father who'd come to see them.

Standing in the doorway, holding a heap of peanut-butter-and-banana-sandwich bits, was an eight-foot-tall, 500-pound Sasquatch.

"Crikey," Maddie gulped.

Bigfoot stuffed a handful of sandwich bits in his mouth and watched the Mattigans.

"I don't know what to do," Maddie whispered out of

the side of her mouth.

The Mattigans couldn't move.

Max and Theo were too scared even to talk. Chasing a Sasquatch that was running away from you was one thing — especially when it was only a head on a stick. Standing face-to-face with a real one in your house: well, that was quite another.

The Sasquatch kept stuffing sandwich bits into his mouth until they were gone. Then he held out two massive, hairy paws.

No one knew what to do.

"Uh, Maddie?" Max said. "Look."

Maddie saw. Through the open door, a taxi could be seen coming up the road toward their house.

"Double crikey," Maddie gulped. "This is not good. This is very much *not good.*"

The Sasquatch sniffed the air. Then he lumbered right past the petrified kids into the living room.

Bigfoot approached the window bench that Theo had been hiding in before their lives were turned upside down. He sniffed it. Then he put his paws on it. After a brief investigation, he figured out how to lift it open.

Then he grunted, with something that had to be pleasure.

"You left some wedges in there," Max whispered to Theo.

The Sasquatch was leaning deep into the seat now, trying to fish the wedges out.

"Maddie," Theo hissed. Their father was walking up to the house.

That's when Maddie did the craziest thing she'd ever done in her life. She rushed over and shoved Bigfoot as hard as she could. He gave out a grunt of surprise, and then fell into the seat. Maddie slammed the lid down over him.

There then came the sound of more grunting — grunting *and* growling — but it did not come from the Sasquatch. It came from another creature, the one who at that moment stormed through the front door: Marcus Mattigan.

CHAPTER TEN

THE DEAL

"I am so disappointed in you kids!" Marcus snarled. "We need to talk. Right *now.*" He looked completely wiped out. His clothes were a mess, and his crazy hair was a total disaster.

"We have something to tell you!" Maddie said, rushing to her dad.

"Everyone sit down, right now."

"But — !"

"I don't want to hear it. I will do the talking. Now. Everyone, hit the puffy couch."

The Mattigan kids sat in a row.

Marcus sat across from them. He took a deep breath, but before he could get a word out, Theo blurted: "He lied to us! He told us he was your dad! You never showed us pictures of what he looks like! Not even one!"

Marcus's mouth opened, but he seemed unable to say whatever he was planning to say. His shoulders sagged.

No one said anything for a while.

Finally, Max went and got the monster journal from his room and handed it to his father. Marcus flipped through it, looking teary.

"He said that if you could see that one of the monsters was real — just one," Maddie explained, "then you'd understand why he left you."

"And you'd forgive him," Max added.

"Because everyone needs their parents," Theo put in.

Marcus didn't look mad anymore. He looked sad, though — very, very sad.

"Did the real Grandpa Joe really leave you to search for monsters?" Maddie asked.

Marcus nodded.

"How did Ivan Blavatsky know?"

"That's what he does," Marcus explained. "He researches his victims, so he has information that makes them trust him. It's an old, but very effective trick. I talked about my father once in an interview. It's on the Internet for anyone to find."

"Teachable Moment," the kids said for him.

Marcus smiled, but it was the kind of smile that made them all want to cry.

"We have something to tell you, Dad," Maddie tried again. She looked over at the bench. She was pretty sure she heard the sounds of chewing coming from inside it.

Marcus didn't seem to hear it, though. He didn't seem to have heard her, either. "The truth is," he said softly, almost as if he was talking to himself, "I don't think I'd want to know if any of these monsters were real."

"Dad," Maddie tried a third time, "we have something to — wait, *what?"*

"And not just because I'm Marcus Mattigan, *profes-*

65

sional skeptic. Truth is: I'd rather believe my father was crazy than that these monsters were more important to him than I was. I'm sorry, kids — my dad took me aside when I was ten years old and told me that there were rare and mysterious creatures in the universe — *universe,* he said, which shows you just how crazy he was. He said if he didn't find them and look after them, nobody would. He said he was sorry to leave me, but it was his calling in life, and he knew I would be well cared for. And I certainly was, by my mother. But I couldn't understand why she never seemed angry about his leaving us. She always told me he was a good man, and that he'd come back to us, if it were at all possible. But neither of us ever saw him again." Marcus seemed to snap out of a daze just then. "Anyway," he said, looking at Maddie, "what did you want to tell me?"

The kids looked at each other.

"Nothing," all three of them said.

No one knew what to do now.

A loud grunt sounded from the direction of the benches. All three kids cleared their throats to cover it up. Marcus looked at them curiously for a moment, but made no comment. He flipped through the monster journal some more. "People really do think these ridiculous things are real," he said, shaking his head and sounding suddenly much more like himself. "And not just basket cases like my father. They spend hard-earned money on T-shirts and souvenirs and fake evidence. *Millions* of dollars."

"People," the Mattigan kids sighed.

There was another grunt, and then another triple throat-clearing.

"Are you guys getting sick?" Marcus asked. Then he said, mostly to himself, "I think my show will be off the air for a while, or longer. Maybe I need a vacation, anyway." But then he focused on his kids again. "I've been meaning to spend more time with you," he told them. "The last thing I want to do is end up like my father, never seeing my own children."

"It's our fault," Max said, feeling about as bad as he'd ever felt. "I just wish there was something we could to do to fix the problem."

Maddie's eyes lit up. "Maybe we can!" she realized.

"Maybe we could travel around this summer together, on vacation, but also help you with some cases! Why don't we go to Las Vegas and prove that alien escape thing that you told us about is a fake! If it works out, your producer will have to let you make a show out of it, and if not, we'll have a fun trip!"

"Innnteresting," Marcus said, which was a great sign. Max, Maddie and Theo exchanged hopeful looks. Then their father said, "You know what? I think that's a great idea!"

Just then distinct bangs came from the benches.

"Did you hear that?" Marcus said, getting up. He walked toward the giant windows.

"Dad, no!" the kids all cried.

Marcus stopped and looked back at his kids with surprise and worry in his eyes. But then the banging came again.

Marcus reached down and lifted one of the lids.

"NOOOOO!"

"What in the world!"

CHAPTER ELEVEN

REMARKABLY UNDERSTANDING

Marcus had opened the left-side bench — and found Betsy, the kids' sitter, tied up and struggling inside. There was tape over her mouth. The Mattigans helped her out and freed her. Naturally, she was very upset about having been attacked and forced to spend the night in a dark hole — though grateful it was full of pillows.

Once all was explained, she was remarkably understanding, especially after Marcus offered to pay her triple and mention her in his next show, if he ever had one. Even so, and not surprisingly, she wanted to leave as soon as possible. She'd arrived by cab, but Marcus offered to drive her home, and she accepted.

"You Mattigans really are an interesting family," she said.

"If that's our real name," Max said. For reasons even he didn't understand, he said it in the crouch.

"I'll be back soon," Marcus told the kids as he and Betsy headed out. He was in a much better mood now. "You guys know the getting along — "

"Notta fist!" Max cried.

"Notta foot!" Maddie added.

"Notta finger!" Theo concluded.

"Notta problem!" Betsy put in.

"Oklahoma," Marcus told her, as he closed the door behind them.

The Mattigan kids looked at each other. They didn't know what to say. They were excited. Nervous, but excited.

"He wasn't ready," Maddie said.

Her brothers nodded.

Suddenly, the right-side bench flew open and Bigfoot climbed out of it. He was out of sandwiches.

Theo rushed into the kitchen and came back with another bagful.

"How did you — ?" Max asked, amazed.

"Emergency reserves," Theo said.

"Genius!" Maddie took the bag and showed it to the hairy giant, who grunted with pleasure again and took a step toward her. "I'll lead him into the forest through the basement door," she told her brothers, adding, "So nobody sees." She edged backward towards the basement steps, then climbed down one stair. "Come on," she urged. The Sasquatch stepped toward her. "That's a good — Bigfoot."

"*If* that's his real name," Max said.

"I think it's Sasquatch, actually," Theo said.

"Ah-*ha!*"

Maddie backed farther down the stairs. The Sasquatch reached the top, but hesitated. Then, looking not entirely unlike Max in search-mode, he crouched. Maddie turned and hurried down into the basement.

Bigfoot followed.

CHAPTER TWELVE

TRUE STORY

"He wouldn't leave," Maddie said when she reappeared ten minutes later. "He's in a room, eating. I left the back door open, so maybe he'll go out when he's done."

"Maybe he'll stay!" Theo said. He was sitting on the puffy couch next to Max, who had the monster journal open on his lap.

"We're gonna need to go shopping," Max said, without looking up.

Maddie walked over to see what he was doing.

Max had his spy pen in hand. After clicking off its invisible ink mode, he said, "I'm sure Dad will toss this out, and that's probably a good idea. Who knows how much of this stuff is made up. But still — " He found an empty space on the Sasquatch pages and wrote, "Favorite food: peanut-butter-and-banana sandwiches."

"True story!" his brother and sister proclaimed.

Postscript

BIGFOOT!

And that, dear readers, is how it all began. It's quite a story if you think about it. On that note, I have a question for you. Out of everyone who stepped foot in the Mattigan Mansion that weekend, who was the real monster?

Teachable Moment, no?

Discuss among yourselves.

And while you're at it, I'll do my best to prepare the story of the next Mattigan adventure. It's monstrously good, too. I just hope it's not too *out there* for you.

Meanwhile, here's some advice. Keep your basement door open at night, and don't stop leaving those peanut-butter-and-banana sandwiches under the bed.

Sincerely,

Your pal

About The Author

David Michael Slater is an acclaimed author of books for children, teens, and adults. His work for children includes the picture books *Cheese Louise!*, *The Bored Book*, and *The Boy & the Book*, as  well as the on-going teen fantasy series, *Forbidden Books*, which is being developed for film by a former producer of *The Lion King*. David's work for adults includes the hilarious comic-drama, *Fun & Games*, which the New York Journal of Books writes "works brilliantly." David teaches in Reno, Nevada, where he lives with his wife and son. You can learn more about David and his work at www.davidmichaelslater.com.

About Mysterious Monsters

Mysterious Monsters is a humorous six-book early chapter book series full of mystery and adventure. When Marcus Mattigan, star of the popular show "Monstrous Lies with Marcus Mattigan" offers to let his kids, Maddie, Max, and Theo, travel around the country with him as he exposes frauds and fakes, the trio manages to find and capture the world's most mysterious and elusive creatures — and then to hide them in their increasingly crowded basement. As you can imagine, with each book, the situation gets more and more hairy.

Credits

This book is a work of art produced by Incorgnito Publishing Press.

Susan Comninos
Editor

Mauro Sorghienti
Illustrator/Artist

Star Foos
Designer

Janice Bini
Chief Reader

Daria Lacy
Graphic Production

Michael Conant
Publisher

March 2017
Incorgnito Publishing Press